HILDA AND THE MAD SCIENTIST

BY *Addie Adam* ★ PICTURES BY *Lisa Thiesing*

DUTTON CHILDREN'S BOOKS · NEW YORK

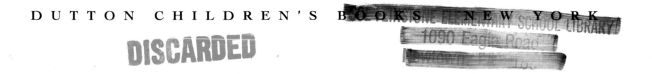

For Cindy and the memories we share
A. A.

To Jan Faust, a real fine teacher
L.T.

Library of Congress Cataloging-in-Publication Data
Adam, Addie
Hilda and the mad scientist/by Addie Adam;
illustrated by Lisa Thiesing.—1st ed.   p. cm.
Summary: When helpful Hilda decides to move in to take care
of the grouchy Dr. Weinerstein, a mad scientist, his efforts
to get rid of her have unexpected results.
ISBN 0-525-45386-5
[1. Behavior—Fiction.   2. Humorous stories.]
I. Thiesing, Lisa, ill.   II. Title.
PZ7.A1865Hi   1995
[E]—dc20   94-33989   CIP   AC

Published in the United States 1995 by Dutton Children's Books,
a division of Penguin Books USA Inc.
375 Hudson Street, New York, New York 10014
Designed by Adrian Leichter
Printed in Hong Kong   First Edition
1 3 5 7 9 10 8 6 4 2

Hilda was loved by one and all. She had big muscles, big feet and, best of all, a big heart. She always said, "People should help people." And she always did. "I go where I'm needed and stay until I'm not," she told everyone.

So she used her big muscles and big feet and helped the baker carry his cakes and pastries to the king. "I go where I'm needed and stay until I'm not," she huffed as she carried the trays up the stairs of the castle.

She helped the butcher, the street sweeper and everyone else who needed her. And when she heard that weird Dr. Weinerstein was suffering from rheumatism all alone in his creepy old mansion up on Vampire Hill, she wanted to help him too. She filled two baskets with food, announcing to the townspeople, "I go where I'm needed and stay until I'm not. I will take care of him until he doesn't need me."

Hilda's friends begged her not to go. "He's a mad scientist," said one. "He makes monsters in that creepy old mansion," said another.

"Fiddle-faddle," Hilda scoffed. "Nobody can make a monster."
And with that, she picked up her baskets of supplies and headed
toward Dr. Weinerstein's dilapidated mansion on the hill.

When she arrived at his door, she wiped her big shoes on the mat and lifted the heavy door knocker.

Bam! Bam! Bam!

The door creaked open with a horrible groan.

Hilda stepped inside. The great hall was filled with dark shadows. "Dr. Weinerstein," she called. "I'm Hilda. I heard you have rheumatism, and so I've come to cook your meals, clean your house and make your rheumatism better."

"Go away," said a spooky voice from somewhere in the darkness.

"Can't," Hilda replied. "I go where I'm needed and stay until I'm not."

She wrinkled her nose at the cobwebs hanging from the chandelier. "And I am certainly needed here!"

Suddenly, a man in a black cape swooshed down the long, curving staircase.

"You really shouldn't slide down banisters in your condition," Hilda scolded.

"I didn't. I flew," Dr. Weinerstein said.

"Fiddle-faddle," Hilda said. "People can't fly. Now show me the way to the kitchen. What you need is a good meal."

"What I need is to be left alone!" he snarled. But Hilda kept right on walking until she found the kitchen. "And if you don't go," he shouted after her, "I have an evil spell to make you disappear."

But Hilda had no time for such nonsense talk. There was work to do. She pulled groceries from her basket and began to cook. Soon the whole house smelled of roast beef and vegetables. She was singing as she finished rolling out the dough for an apple pie. So she did not hear the scientist creeping up behind her. He held a wand over her head and chanted, "Parish Parilda, vaporize Hilda!"

Nothing happened. Hilda held out her big hands covered with flour. "See? I'm still here!"

Dr. Weinerstein stomped away furiously.

Later, he tiptoed up beside her and dropped a spider onto Hilda's pie to frighten her away.

"Poor little thing," Hilda cooed. She carried the spider outside and set it on a rosebush, where it could spin webs and catch bugs.

He grumbled as he watched Hilda use her feather duster to clean away cobwebs over the dining-room table. He blinked like an owl when she threw open the shutters to let in some light. And he sputtered when she chased his pet bat out of the house.

At dinner, when he reached for a piece of apple pie, Hilda made him eat his broccoli first.

She made him brush his teeth — what was left of them —

and go to bed early with a hot-water bottle at his feet.

And to help cure his rheumatism, she made him wear long, woolly socks. They kept his legs warm, but they also made him itch a lot.

Finally, after a week, Dr. Weinerstein had had enough. He clumped up the stairs to his laboratory muttering, "I can see I will have to use my master plan to scare her away."

He chuckled as he looked around his laboratory with its flasks of purple pompom poison, thick brown swamp mud, powdered bat-bane, deadly yellow chokedamp, black eel eyes and white snail tails. "Now all I need is my monster-making machine from the roof. I'll just go up and get it."

He flew up the back stairs as Hilda climbed up the front steps carrying a mop, a bucket and a feather duster.

She stepped inside the laboratory. "Oh, what a mess! What a smell!" she exclaimed.

She sniffed the flask of purple pompom poison. "This grape juice is spoiled." She smelled the other flasks and wrinkled her nose. "Everything in here is spoiled. I'll have to get rid of it all and bring up some nice fresh food from the kitchen." So she did. Soon the flasks held grape juice, chocolate milk, corn starch, lemon soda, raisins and macaroni.

But the mad scientist didn't know that! As Dr. Weinerstein low-
ered himself down through the roof with his monster-making
machine, Hilda was just leaving the laboratory.

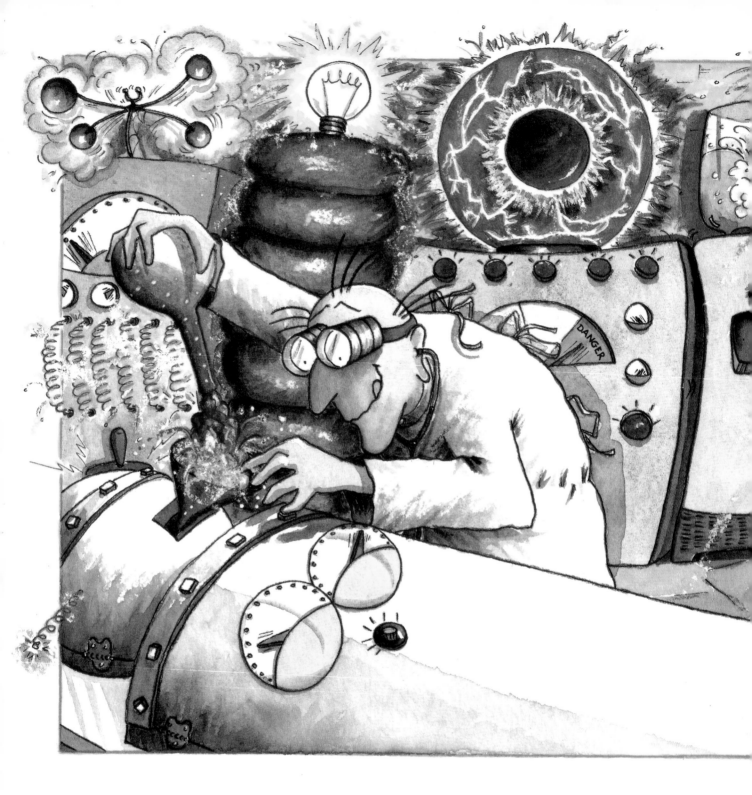

The scientist mixed, stirred and chuckled. "Now I will make my monster. It will be my scariest ever! It will frighten Hilda out of her wits — and out of my house!"

He dumped the potion into the machine. The lights blinked off and on, and sparks flew around the room.

"Finished!" the mad scientist shrieked when the machine stopped sparking. "Now it's good-bye, Hilda!"

At that moment, Hilda, who had been mopping the stairs, appeared in the doorway. "Did I hear you say 'good night, Hilda'?" She looked at the clock. "You're right. It is time for bed."

"I told you to go, but you would not listen," the scientist growled. "Now I have made a dreadful, scary monster to chase you away." "Fiddle-faddle," Hilda scoffed. "Nobody can make a monster."

But her eyes widened as she watched the scientist pull open the top of his machine. On a slab inside lay a great bundle wrapped in bandages.

He started to unwind them.

First the feet appeared.

"Your monster's feet are big like mine," she said, admiring her own big feet.

"A dreadful, scary monster has to have big feet," the scientist snapped.

He unwound more. Hilda smiled. "How nice. A monster in a dress. And it's just like mine! Do all your monsters wear dresses?"

"Something's wrong with the recipe," the scientist muttered and began to sweat.

He unwrapped faster.

Finally, the bandages were off, and there it was —

THE MONSTER!

Hilda was so pleased! "How clever you are! You did make a monster, and it looks just like me! Now I can go back to town to see where I'm needed next. And you will always have someone here to make you take your naps and wear your woolly socks."

She didn't understand why Dr. Weinerstein was screaming.

At the door, Hilda turned to wave good-bye, but the very mad scientist did not notice. He was staring at his monster, who was cleaning up the laboratory. She made long, busy sweeps with her big arms. Flasks flew through the air and crashed on the floor.

Hilda sighed contentedly. "I go where I'm needed and stay until I'm not," she said to herself as she walked back into town. Now she would never have to worry about Dr. Weinerstein. He would always have someone to take care of him.

E
A   Adam, Addie.

          Hilda and the mad
          scientist.

$14.99

DATE			